My Sister, My Friend

My Sister, My Friend — A Review

by Neil L. Yuzuk

Editor of the children's book, "The Legend of the Smiling Chihuahua" and
The author of the adult book series, "Beachside PD."

When I first met Barbara Dominick she was a trainer and I was a counselor for the SPARK Program—a substance abuse prevention and intervention program in New York City high schools. There was always respect and warmth between us as the job, quite often, could be heartbreakingly difficult—saving young lives.

Fast forward to 2015 and I am now living in Los Angeles, retired and working as an author, and Barbara is still in the business of saving lives, now through her ministry and writing.

In Barbara Dominick's short story, "My Sister, My Friend," the after-school day turns unpleasant between two sisters, Jill and Chris when Chris discovers Jill misbehaving and threatens to tell their mother. But when, minutes later, it is Chris who is at the mercy of Jill, they need to come to a truce or they will both feel their mother's anger.

"My Sister, My Friend" is a simple story gloriously told . . . and yet, despite its simplicity, it is an in-depth look at the fragile bond between siblings. It is a morality tale for children of all ages.

My Sister, My Friend

by
Barbara Dominick

Balboa Press books may be ordered through booksellers or by contacting:

Balboa Press
A Division of Hay House
1663 Liberty Drive
Bloomington, IN 47403
www.balboapress.com
1 (877) 407-4847

Because of the dynamic nature of the Internet, any web addresses or links contained in this book may have changed since publication and may no longer be valid. The views expressed in this work are solely those of the author and do not necessarily reflect the views of the publisher, and the publisher hereby disclaims any responsibility for them.

Any people depicted in stock imagery provided by Thinkstock are models, and such images are being used for illustrative purposes only.
Certain stock imagery © Thinkstock.

ISBN: 978-1-5043-5543-8 (sc)
ISBN: 978-1-5043-5542-1 (e)

Library of Congress Control Number: 2016906571

Print information available on the last page.

Balboa Press rev. date: 06/25/2016

BALBOA
PRESS
A DIVISION OF HAY HOUSE

For Vicki, my eternal Soul-Sister.

To my sons Kahlil and BeyNamaan; my grandchildren
and great-grandchildern: Gregory, Taryn, Kahlila,
Gabrielle, Tajhi, Kahlil Jr., Nia, Jemire, Christian, Cayden,
Miyla, Marcus and more on their way to meet me.

Deepest gratitude to Infinite Source, Isabel Byron, Victoria
Dennis, Beverly Ewan, Cathy Facciola, Claire Furano and
Neil Yuzuk for the love, support and encouragement.

It was a cold winter day, so cold that everything seemed frozen. Last night's storm had left a heavy blanket of snow that covered the city and muffled all sound. The streets were empty and even the Milbank School, on Lenox Avenue and 117th Street in Harlem, NY, seemed strangely quiet. The school was always buzzing with the sound of the children's voices. But, today there seemed to be no children inside.

Suddenly, they came bolting through the doors. There were children coming from every direction onto the snow-filled street. They were screaming with the sounds of joy—FREEDOM.

They had been locked in the auditorium for assembly and now each grade was being released, one at a time. The fifth grade was the first to come out. After putting in six hours of labor, these hard-working fifth graders were free. They could either stop for a snack with some friends or go home and wrestle with chores and homework. Yet, they chose to remain.

As they gaily danced about in the soft carpet of snow, an object went flying through the air and crash landed on a girl with pigtails.

Another followed, catching a boy on his leg, causing his knee to buckle. The air was filled with snowball traffic coming from every direction.

Children's arms were swinging as they threw their hastily-made snowballs. Their legs were pumping while they dodged incoming missiles—it was heavy snowball combat.

The girl in pigtails had positioned herself behind a pile of snow. She had her snowballs all lined up—she was ready for revenge. At two second intervals she would poke her head up to make sure everything was clear. Then she would take aim, shoot, and duck. She was an expert; she always hit her target. In the confusion of battle, no one was aware of her. There was too much going on. So she continued to pop up . . . aim . . . throw . . . and duck. Pop up . . . aim . . . throw . . . and duck. SPLAT!

The school bully caught it right in the face. He looked about to see where the snowball came from but with everyone throwing snowballs he couldn't tell. He turned and bent down to make a snowball. When he rose, just as he was about to get it in the face again, he spied the pigtailed girl with her pile of snowballs.

The girl behind the embankment was unaware that she had struck twice in the same place and that it was the school bully. She went on with confidence, setting up her stash in preparation for the next opening. As she got up and drew her arm back for a perfect throw, she saw a storm of snowballs whizzing through the air moving fast towards her.

The barrage was coming at her with lightning speed . . . there was no time to duck for cover . . . she was pounded by one snowball after another. She tried to reach for her stash but there were so many snowballs coming at her at the same time that she lost her footing. She fell head-on into a soft mound of snow. As she fell she could hear a voice in the distance calling her name.

"Jill, Jill."

She tried to pick herself up, but the school bully and his friends had no mercy. When she finally managed to get to her feet, everyone was standing—looking and laughing at her. She was covered with snow. Her pigtails were undone. The snow on her head began to melt and her hair started to frizz and get really thick. Her unbuttoned coat hung loosely on her small frame. The middy blouse that was starch ironed that morning was wrinkled and only partially tucked into her pants. As she pulled at her knee socks, that had fallen like rags around her ankles, she could see her sister coming toward her.

"Look at you!" she said, grabbing Jill by the collar.

"Just look at you! Why didn't you wear your boots?"

"I forgot!" Jill answered defiantly.

Shaking her finger at Jill, her sister threatened, "Forgot? I guess you forgot to go right home after school too! I'm telling Ma. You wait till she sees you. You're gonna get it."

She knew her sister probably would tell their mother. Chris was only three years older than Jill, yet she acted like a mother.

"Come on, let's go," Chris commanded. "And fix your clothes, you're a . . ." Chris stopped short, she made a fist and gave Jill a swift shot in the arm. "Who said you could wear my blouse? I told you about wearing my clothes! That's my best blouse, now it's ruined."

Chris grabbed Jill by the arm and shook her silly. "Fix your clothes," she snapped.

Jill could see the anger in her sister's face. She could only reply, "I'm fixing them, I'm fixing them."

"If Ma was here she would really be upset and fuss at you, maybe even discipline you out here."

Chris wasn't about to let up. "Just wait till you get home," she insisted.

Jill knew she would have to suffer Chris's mental torture on the short trip home. Even if their mother didn't fuss or discipline her for her conduct in the schoolyard, Chris was sure letting her have it with the lip switch. Jill was used to her older sister, so she closed her mind to the sounds coming from her.

They lived on 120th Street and Fifth Avenue, only four blocks from the school. Jill had to think of a way to prevent her sister from telling their mother and she had to think fast. Three of the four blocks home were short ones.

As they walked up Lenox Avenue in the stillness of the cold afternoon, Jill could see people shoveling snow, clearing the sidewalks. Cars were going by slowly, making slush out of the snow that had just been white feathery flakes. The chains on the back wheels of cars reminded Jill of the time their father took them into the country for a sleigh ride. The sound also brought warm thoughts of Christmas. She could see Kris Kringle riding across her mind in his sleigh.

A man ran past them. When he tried to cross the street, he lost his footing. He fell. This gave Jill a start. She realized they were on 118th Street. Almost home and my time was running out, she thought.

Chris was still going on. Somehow she had gotten on the subject of why it was so important to act like a nice girl. Ha, whatever that is, Jill thought!

"Acting wild just isn't ladylike," she was saying.

"Chris," Jill interrupted, "Why can't I have fun and still be a nice girl?"

"You call getting beat up in a snowball fight having fun?" she asked. But, she wasn't really looking for an answer. Chris continued, "That's for those rough boys, not you."

Jill asked again, "Why can't I have fun and still be a nice girl?"

Chris was silent, as though she had to think very hard about the answer.

She sucked her teeth and said, "You just don't know how to behave."

Jill figured her sister didn't know herself why it was so important. As far as Jill knew, there was nothing more important than having fun. When you're all grown up the fun seems to stop. Grown up people don't hardly ever seem to laugh. Maybe they forget how to have fun. Their mother didn't laugh anymore either. Jill's favorite name for her mother was ol' stoneface. She giggled to herself when she thought of when her mother would finally laugh. Someday ol' stoneface would crack a smile and her face would fall to the floor in a million pieces.

Jill and Chris were now approaching 119th Street. The store fronts were being cleared of snow. As Jill and her sister tracked snow onto the cleaned pavement she thought it was time to plead her case.

"I'll do the dishes for a whole week if you don't tell," Jill said.

"What?"

Jill repeated, "Ok, so, I'll do the dishes for a whole month if you don't tell.

Chris looked at her in amazement. "Now you're trying to bribe me? You just get worse by the minute, don't you!" she answered.

"PLEASE," Jill begged.

"Forget it," was Chris's response.

Jill thought, *'I could really beat you up Chris. Bury you under a whole lot of snow and they wouldn't find you till morning.'* Instead she said, "So why do you have to tell? I didn't get hurt or anything."

Chris was insistent. "I'm going to tell anyway. I'm the oldest and I'm supposed to look out for you and make sure you do the right thing."

"Oh, yeah, right. And, who makes sure you do the right thing?" Jill wanted to know.

"If you were really looking out for me, you would have helped me get that bully in the school yard. And you wouldn't tell Ma either." Jill was hoping she was getting through to her sister.

Chris made a movement with her hand as though she was cutting through the air and said in a loud frustrated voice, "FORGET IT!"

"You're a witch," Jill was pouting. "I wish you weren't my sister."

"Keep it up. Ma is gonna have a lot of reasons to punish you tonight. And you know how she is when she gets to that," Chris threatened.

Well punishment could be anything from extra chores to not being able to go out and play. What she really didn't want was her mother going to the school to have a meeting with the Principal and the bully's parents. What an embarrassment that would be.

When they got to the corner of Lenox Avenue and 119th Street, they could see the neighborhood kids in the next block making a snowman.

Mr. Watson, the local grocer was shoveling snow and fussing at the kids for making a mess. They teased and danced around him. When Jill and Chris came onto the block Mr. Watson called to the kids, "You see these nice girls," he said while pointing to Jill and Chris. "They have manners and they respect older people. They see me shoveling snow, they won't make a mess for me. Right girls?"

Mr. Watson was a nice man. He loved the kids in the neighborhood. Fussing was his way of having fun with them, and teaching kids to be responsible.

Jill answered, "Yes, Mr. Watson." But she would like more than anything to be with the other kids helping to make a snowman, and yes, making a mess right along with them.

The kids making the snowman stopped and eyed each other first, then altogether they began cleaning the mess and offered to help Mr. Watson finish shoveling his snow. To Jill, even that would be fun.

Jill could see Mr. Watson was pleased. He turned to Chris and asked, "How was school today, Chris?"

"Fine, thank you, Mr. Watson," she answered.

Mr. Watson went on. "You know, you girls are so nice and loving to one another . . . you're more like friends. I had two sisters and they were always fighting. But, you two," he nodded his head, "really look out for each other. That's nice, really nice."

Jill eyed her sister and wished that what Mr. Watson was saying could be true. Chris just stood there smiling.

Jill was beginning to feel the cold. She said, "Mr. Watson, we have to be going now."

"Yeah," Chris chimed in, "We have to be going."

"I have to get back to my work too. You girls have a nice day," he said.

The two sisters started walking again and Jill thought she might try her luck one more time. "Did you hear what Mr. Watson said about us being loving?"

"Yes, so what," Chris snapped.

Jill asked, "Do you think telling Ma is being loving?"

"Look, I don't care what you say. You weren't supposed to be out there playing in the snow. No boots and with my good blouse on, too." They turned the corner of 120th Street. It was a long block, but Jill realized it would be the shortest walk ever.

"Chris, I . . ."

"NO." Chris was abrupt.

Frustrated, Jill stuffed her right hand into her pocket. Although the inside of the pocket was ragged and frayed, she began nervously pulling at the loose threads. Pretty soon she could get three fingers through the hole in the seam.

Suddenly, Chris blurted out, "O, I forgot something. Ma wanted us to bring some eggs home with us." She reached into her bag for the money.

"Here, you go back and get the eggs."

Jill's entire hand tore right through the seam in her pocket and made a gigantic hole.

"You just want me to go so you could have time to tell Ma what I did." Jill's voice was shaking.

Chris gave her a threatening look and said, "Jill, just go to the store. Okay?"

Her last hope gone Jill turned and ran back to Mr. Watson's store. She was fuming all the way.

When she got back to the store she saw all the kids had gone except for one girl. She was trying to finish the snowman. Mr. Watson was inside waiting on a woman wearing a pretty red coat and yellow beads hanging outside the coat. He was trying to explain to her that he didn't stock the item she was asking for. "There just wasn't enough demand for it," he said.

The woman then sent him to his stock room… "Just to make sure," she told him.

Jill wondered how long it would take. While Mr. Watson was gone, Jill's mind began to wander again. She imagined that Chris was already upstairs telling their mother all about the snowball fight.

By the time Jill got home her mother would be waiting. She'd open the door, and there would be that all familiar stone-faced look on her face that meant 'Now you've gone and done it, you're in deep trouble'. Her mother's lips would be pushed toward the left side of her face. The teeth would be nipping away at the inside of her right cheek and her foot would be nervously tapping out a fast angry beat. Jill could see it all . . . and then the long lecture followed by an even longer list of punishments.

"I'm sorry, I don't have it." Mr. Watson's voice abruptly brought Jill's mind back to the present moment. The woman in the red coat threw her head back, stuck her nose up in the air, and walked out of the store in a huff.

"Mr. Watson, Mr. Watson," Jill desperately called to Mr. Watson.

Stumbling over her words, she said, "Can I have a dozen eggs please."

"Sure." Mr. Watson went to his dairy, and to Jill's relief he immediately came back with the eggs.

Jill had the paper bag ready and the money on the counter. It was the exact change so she didn't have to wait. She stuffed the eggs in the bag and dashed out of the store with hardly a polite "Goodbye."

Jill ran as fast as she could. She held on tightly to the eggs and was careful not to crush them. She zipped around the corner of 120th Street in a flash. Now the block looked like it stretched until forever. She wasn't getting home fast enough.

When finally she reached her building, she stopped in the hallway to catch her breath. Suddenly, she heard voices coming from behind the staircase. She listened closely. Jill heard her sister saying, "I have to go. Jill will be coming any minute now. I'll meet you here tomorrow afternoon."

Jill walked behind the staircase and saw Chris kissing Derek, the neighborhood nerd, on the cheek. With emphasis, Jill broke the silence.

"CHRIS, I got the eggs."

Chris and her companion were so startled they jumped. Derek's caramel brown complexion turned three shades darker. Chris tried to speak, but she stuttered so nervously Jill could not understand her.

Jill thought what a pretty picture this would be for their mother to see. She didn't say another word, she simply walked around to the first landing to wait for her sister. There was no doubt in her mind what would happen if their mother found out about her sister's behavior.

Derek was the first to come out from behind the stairs. As he walked down the hall and out the door, Jill looked around to see her sister staring at her.

"Well, are you going to tell?" Chris asked.

Jill just eyed her sister and said in a hard tone, "Let's go."

They climbed the three flights of stairs to their apartment without a word. The silence was the loudest thing Jill could hear. *What a moment,* she thought, *now I have the power and it'll be Chris getting punished.*

When they got to their floor Chris turned and desperately asked again. "Are you going to tell Ma?"

Before Jill could answer, the door to their apartment swung open. Their mother was standing there with her arms folded and a stern look on her face. Jill heard the foot tapping on the floor. It was the familiar 'You're in trouble' beat.

"What took you girls so long to get home?" their mother asked.

Jill and Chris entered the apartment. Jill gave the eggs to her mother and waited for her sister to answer.

Chris hesitated before answering. She looked in Jill's direction—Jill was putting her books down and taking off her coat. Their eyes met.

"We forgot the eggs, so we had to go back to the store," said Chris.

Their mother looked at them, her suspicious mind was working, "Are you two alright? You act as if something is wrong. Did anything happen in school today."

Again Chris answered. "No, everything is okay." She looked at Jill and asked, "Right, Jill?"

Jill smiled and said, "Right, everything is okay Ma, we're just fine."

The next morning Jill got up early and went into her sister's room. "Here's your blouse, Chris."

Jill had washed and bleached it the night before. Now it was on a hanger pressed and ready to wear. Chris looked her sister in the eyes and gave her a warm smile.

She leaned toward Jill, kissed her on the cheek and said, "It really doesn't fit me anymore. You can have it Jill."

A surprised Jill said, "Really! Wow, thanks Chris."

Chris asked, "By the way, who was that boy yesterday, he had everyone throwing snowballs at you?"

Jill said, "That's the school bully. His name is Barry Brown."

"I thought so. Well, guess what. Derek knows his brother. And, we'll meet you after school tomorrow."

"You will?!" Jill was so excited.

"Yes," Chris said. "I have to look out for you, right. After all you're not just my sister, you're my best friend, and I love you."

Jill was glowing, she thought, *'Wow, what's better than your own sister being your best friend. And, Derek is probably not so bad after all.'*

Jill grabbed and held her sister in a loving embrace, and said, "Thanks Sis, I love you too."

It was a heartfelt hug that left them with a warm tingling sensation.

Chris smiled lovingly at Jill and said, "My sister!"

Jill could feel a smile on her own heart as she said, "My friend!"

They would always look back to this moment, the moment when they bonded as sisters and friends. It's the story they tell their children and grandchildren.

CPSIA information can be obtained
at www.ICGtesting.com
Printed in the USA
BVOW07s2158070716

454851BV00008B/11/P